MAYWOOD PUBLIC LIBRARY
121 SOUTH 5th AVE.
MAYWOOD, ILL. 60153

JOSIE SMITH

Magdalen Nabb
illustrations by Pirkko Vainio

Margaret K. McElderry Books
NEW YORK

Margaret K. McElderry Books
Macmillan Publishing Company
866 Third Avenue
New York, NY 10022

First published in 1988 by William Collins Sons & Co Ltd
First United States Edition 1989

Printed in the United States of America

10 9 8 7 6 5 4 3 2 1

Library of Congress Cataloging-in-Publication Data
Nabb, Magdalen, 1947-
Josie Smith.
Summary: Follows the amusing misadventures of a little girl as she shops for the perfect birthday gift for her mother, blackens a blackboard, and cares for a lost cat.
[1. Mothers and daughters—Fiction] I. Vainio, Pirkko, ill. II. Title.
PZ7.N125Jo 1989 [Fic] 88-8301
ISBN 0-689-50485-3

Contents

JOSIE SMITH and the BIRTHDAY FLOWERS

On Saturday morning it rained and rained and in the afternoon it stopped.

Josie Smith stood on one leg and pulled her sock up. Then she stood on the other leg and pulled her other sock up. Then she put on her rubber boots and her blue jacket.

"Put a hat on!" shouted Josie Smith's mom from the kitchen, "and tie your scarf properly!"

Josie Smith pulled a horrible face. She put on a wooly hat that itched and a wooly scarf that itched even more, winding it round and round so that she wouldn't get tonsillitis.

Every time she went out, her mom said,

"If you don't tie that scarf properly, you'll end up with tonsillitis."

Josie Smith went out and shut the door behind her. Josie's house was number 1. It was the same as all the other houses in the street and the street was the same as all the other streets on the side of the hill and on the top of the hill there was a tower. At the bottom of the hill was Josie Smith's school and the main road and the shops and the mills with tall chimneys.

Josie Smith saw Eileen next door sitting on the step nursing a doll wrapped in a shawl.

"Are you playing?" Eileen said.

"No, I'm not," said Josie Smith. "I'm busy."

"No you're not," said Eileen.

"Yes I am," said Josie Smith. "It's my mom's birthday and I'm going to get her a present and a birthday card."

"I bet you've got no money," Eileen said.

"Yes I have," said Josie Smith.

"You haven't."

"I have. I've got fifty cents," said Josie Smith.

"You're a liar," Eileen said, rocking her doll backwards and forwards. "My mom says I'm not to play with you, because you tell lies."

"I don't want to play with you anyway," Josie Smith said. "You and your stupid doll." And she went off down the street making as much noise as she could with her rubber boots. When she passed Gary Grimes's house, he came to the door. He had on a gray cardigan with a zip up the front and gray slippers with zips up the front as well.

"I can't play outside," Gary Grimes said. "I've got bronchitis, but we can play inside if you want."

"I'm not playing," Josie Smith said. "It's my mom's birthday and I'm going to get her a present and a birthday card."

She waited to see if Gary Grimes would say she hadn't got any money, like Eileen, but Gary Grimes went in and shut the door.

Josie Smith went on down the street making a noise with her boots. The pavements were wet and in the big puddles she could see dirty clouds going past the upside-down chimneys but it didn't start raining. At the end of the street was the spare ground where there was grass and cinders and the things that people threw away. Josie Smith searched all over the grass and all over the cinders looking for bottles to take back to the shop. It wasn't really a lie when she told Eileen she had fifty cents, because she was going to get it soon. Josie Smith found two small bottles in the grass and a big bottle that was nearly buried in the cinders. She had to dig for it with a stick. She held the bottles tight against her chest and carried them to Mrs. Chadwick's shop.

"I've brought these back," she said, and put them up on the counter.

Mrs. Chadwick looked mad.

"Josie Smith!" she shouted. "Look at all the dirt you've put on my counter!"

Josie Smith reached up and tried to rub the dirt away with her sleeve but Mrs. Chadwick still looked mad. She was holding the big bottle between two fingers and pulling a funny face.

"Those other two should be thrown away," Mrs. Chadwick said. "They're not returnable. But I suppose I can give you something on this. What do you want today? Chocolate bars or Gummi Bears?"

"I don't want Gummi Bears today," Josie Smith said. "It's my mom's birthday and I'm going to get her a present and a birthday card."

"Here then," said Mrs. Chadwick. "You can give her this." And she held out a bun with white icing on it and a cherry on top.

"I don't want that," said Josie Smith.

"My mom buys cakes on Saturdays. I'm buying her some flowers because she hasn't got any."

Mrs. Chadwick got some money from the cash register and put it on the counter. Josie Smith reached up for it.

"Thank you, Mrs. Chadwick!" she shouted, and ran out of the shop.

"Wait a minute!" shouted Mrs. Chadwick behind her, but Josie Smith couldn't wait and she ran away. She ran and ran until there were no more houses and she came to Mr. Scowcroft's allotment garden. Mr. Scowcroft had cabbages in his garden and a shed with hens. Mr. Scowcroft was standing amongst the cabbages with his pipe in his mouth, looking at the sky.

"It'll come on to rain again in a while," Mr. Scowcroft said.

"How do you know?" asked Josie Smith. But Mr. Scowcroft didn't say anything. He just made a whistling noise with his pipe.

"Do you want me to dig a bit for you, Mr. Scowcroft?" asked Josie Smith.

"Girls can't dig," Mr. Scowcroft said, still looking at the sky, "not so well as boys can."

"I can dig," said Josie Smith.

"And then there's the worms," Mr. Scowcroft said. "You have to collect the worms you find to give to the hens. Girls don't like worms."

"I like worms, Mr. Scowcroft," Josie Smith said, shutting her eyes as she said it, because it was a lie.

"Well," said Mr. Scowcroft, "we'll see how you do." And he gave her a big spade and a can for the worms.

Josie Smith began to dig. She put her boot on the edge of the spade as she'd seen Mr. Scowcroft do but the spade didn't go in. She stood on the spade with both boots and then it went in. Josie Smith dug and dug and when she saw a worm she bent down and put it in the can, keeping her eyes almost closed so she wouldn't see how much it wriggled. At first, when she started digging, she felt cold, but then she felt hotter and hotter. She took off the itchy scarf and hung it on the fence.

"Why don't the hens get their own worms, Mr. Scowcroft?" she asked.

"They'd peck at my cabbages," Mr. Scowcroft said, "if I let them out."

Josie Smith dug and dug until she couldn't dig anymore.

"I have to go now, Mr. Scowcroft," she said.

"Yes," said Mr. Scowcroft, and he went inside his hen shed.

Josie Smith waited. Was he not going to give her any wages? He always gave the boys wages when they dug.

"Mr. Scowcroft!" shouted Josie Smith. "It's my mom's birthday and I have to get her a present and a birthday card."

Mr. Scowcroft came out. "Birthday is it?" he said. "She'll have a nice birthday surprise when she sees how black you've got yourself. Here." Mr. Scowcroft held out his hand. There were two eggs on it. "You can give these to your mom," he said. "Two brown eggs with red speckles. New laid. That's a nice present."

"I don't want them," Josie Smith said. "My mom buys eggs on Saturdays. I'm buying her some flowers because she hasn't got any."

Mr. Scowcroft sucked on his pipe and made a whistling noise, but he didn't say anything. Then he pulled some coins out of his pants pocket and held them out.

"Thank you, Mr. Scowcroft!" shouted Josie Smith, and she started running.

"Hoy!" shouted Mr. Scowcroft. "Hoy! Wait a minute!"

But Josie Smith was frightened that he might change his mind about the wages and she ran away as fast as she could.

When she was out of breath, she stopped and sat down on the doorstep of Mr. Kefford's fruit and vegetable shop and emptied the dirt out of her rubber boots and pulled her socks up. Then she counted her money. Thirty cents. It wasn't enough. The door of the shop opened behind her.

"What do you think you're doing?" said Mr. Kefford. "Sunbathing?"

"No," said Josie Smith. "It's cold."

"Cold?" said Mr. Kefford. "Rubbish!

Sun's cracking the pavement. Up you get now. I have to sweep out."

"D'you want me to sweep out for you?" asked Josie Smith.

"If you know how to do it properly."

"I'm a good sweeper," Josie Smith said. "I sweep hard."

"Right, then," said Mr. Kefford. "Let's see what you can do."

Josie Smith started to sweep. She swept up cabbage leaves and a sprout and a bit of parsley and a lot of brown dust from the

potatoes, and she shoveled it all into the bag that Mr. Kefford gave her.

"Well," said Mr. Kefford, "you're no bigger than a rabbit but you're a good little sweeper and no mistake. I'd better give you some wages." And he looked round his shop.

"It's my mom's birthday," Josie Smith said. "And I want to get her a present and a birthday card."

She waited, looking up at Mr. Kefford who was very tall and had big red hands with black cracks in them.

"Well, now, let's see..." said Mr. Kefford, and he went to get something from a crate. "Here you are," he said. "You can take this home for your mom." And he held out a big red shiny apple.

"I don't want that," said Josie Smith. "My mom buys apples every Saturday. I want to get her some flowers because she hasn't got any."

"I see," said Mr. Kefford. "I see. That's how it is, is it." Mr. Kefford's big red hand went inside the pocket of his green overalls and pulled out some coins. Josie Smith took the money and ran out of the shop shouting, "Thank you, Mr. Kefford!"

"Hoy!" shouted Mr. Kefford. "Hoy, wait a minute!"

But Josie Smith was running down the street as fast as she could. When she was out of breath she stopped and counted her money. Fifty cents! She started running again and ran until she got to the flower shop. It was getting dark and the light was on in the flower shop window. Josie Smith stood with her nose pressed to the glass, choosing. While she was choosing she stamped her feet in her rubber boots because they were freezing cold. There were all sorts of flowers in the window, pink ones, yellow ones, blue ones, and even some with stripes. But the best flowers were the ones right in the middle. Great big red roses in a white vase. Josie Smith opened the door and went in.

Mrs. Crawshaw was behind the counter, sweeping up leaves.

"I want some flowers for my mom's birthday," said Josie Smith.

"Flowers cost a lot of money in winter,"

Mrs. Crawshaw said, and she went on sweeping up.

"I've got a lot of money," said Josie Smith.

"Have you, now?" said Mrs. Crawshaw, putting down her brush. "Well, which flowers do you want?"

"Roses," said Josie Smith, "those big ones in the window."

Mrs. Crawshaw went to the window and lifted up the big vase. Josie Smith held her breath.

"How many?" asked Mrs. Crawshaw.

"*All* of them," said Josie Smith, putting her pile of money on the counter.

"All of them?" said Mrs. Crawshaw. "Are you sure?"

"Yes," said Josie Smith. "They're for my mom."

"Aren't you Lucy Smith's little girl?" asked Mrs. Crawshaw.

"Yes," said Josie Smith.

"Josie, isn't it?"

"Yes," said Josie Smith.

"Well, Josie," said Mrs. Crawshaw, "I'm afraid these roses cost one dollar."

"Oh..." said Josie Smith. "Oh...I've only got fifty cents, so I can't buy all of them." She thought for a minute, doing a sum in her head. Then she said, "I'll take half the bunch, then."

"No, Josie," said Mrs. Crawshaw. "These roses cost a dollar each. I can't give you half a rose, can I?"

"A dollar each...?" Josie Smith's face went all hot and a lump came into her throat.

"What about a miniature cactus?" said Mrs. Crawshaw, holding out a pot the size of an egg cup with a horrible little green lump in it.

Josie Smith ran to the door, holding her breath so she wouldn't cry.

"Wait!" shouted Mrs. Crawshaw. "Just a minute! Josie!"

But Josie didn't turn around. She ran and ran until she was out of breath, and then she stopped under a lamppost and dried her eyes on her sleeve and wondered what to do. How could flowers cost a dollar each when you only had to pick them? You didn't have to make them; they just grew, like apples. Then she remembered the big red shiny apple. The apple was better than nothing, and the sky was so dark now that it must be late. If she didn't go home soon she'd get into trouble. Josie Smith ran all the way back to Mr. Kefford's fruit and vegetable shop.

"Mr. Kefford! Mr. Kefford!" she shouted, banging on the door. But the door was locked and the lights were off. Mr. Kefford's shop was shut. Josie Smith stood on Mr. Kefford's doorstep, wondering what to do. Then she remembered the big brown eggs with red speckles and she ran all the way back to Mr. Scowcroft's allotment garden.

"Mr. Scowcroft! Mr. Scowcroft!" she shouted, rattling the gate. But it was so dark that she couldn't see the cabbages, and the door of the hen shed was shut. The wind whistled round the garden, but there was no Mr. Scowcroft whistling through his pipe. Mr. Scowcroft had gone home.

Josie Smith stood in the dark near Mr. Scowcroft's garden, wondering what to do. Then she remembered the bun with the

white icing and the cherry on top. She started running and ran all the way back to Mrs. Chadwick's shop.

"Mrs. Chadwick! Mrs. Chadwick!" shouted Josie Smith, banging on the door. But the door was locked and the lights were out. Mrs. Chadwick's shop was shut.

Josie Smith ran home, crying.

"Where have you been till this time?" shouted Josie Smith's mom. "And look at your hands and face and your coat! You're filthy! And where's your scarf? If you've been out without your scarf—"

"I haven't," said Josie Smith.

"Well, where is it, then?"

Josie Smith couldn't remember. She tried her best to remember but she couldn't. She washed her face and hands and sat down at the table. She was hungry and thirsty but before she could start to eat anything she saw on the mantelpiece a big pink birthday card that somebody had sent to her mom. She hadn't even got her mom a card and all the shops were shut. Then she remembered that even when the shops opened again she couldn't buy a card because she'd left all her money on the counter in the flower shop. The lump in Josie Smith's throat got bigger and bigger until she thought she was going to burst. She tried to drink some tea but it was hot and her face was hot and she couldn't drink the tea because if she stopped holding her breath she would cry. Her arms hurt from digging and sweeping and her legs hurt from running too much and the lump in her throat was so big now that it made her feel sick.

"What's the matter now?" said Josie Smith's mom. "You haven't eaten a thing."

"My throat hurts," said Josie Smith in a tiny voice.

"What did I tell you?" Josie Smith's mom was really mad now. "You will go out without your scarf and now you've got tonsillitis!"

Josie Smith was sent to bed.

She hid under the bedclothes until the lump in her throat went away and then she got out of bed and switched the light on. She got her crayons from the windowsill and a piece of paper to fold up and make into a birthday card. Then she sat on the bed and started crayoning. On the front of the card she crayoned a big bunch of red roses in a white vase. Then she thought for a bit and then she crayoned a red and white spotted ribbon round the white vase. Inside the card she crayoned a bun with white icing on it and a cherry on top and two brown eggs with red speckles and a shiny red apple. Then she wrote HAPPY BIRTHDAY MOM, with each letter in a different color.

Downstairs somebody knocked at the front door. *Bam bam bam!*

Josie Smith looked up and listened. She heard a voice. Mrs. Chadwick's voice. Mrs. Chadwick had come to tell on her for dirtying the counter! Josie Smith crept to the top of the stairs in her striped pajamas and sat down on the top step to listen. She couldn't hear all the words, but she heard, "Dirt and cinders all over the counter...," then some words she couldn't hear, and then, "But she ran off before I could catch her." Then the door banged. Mrs. Chadwick had gone away.

Well, now Josie Smith would get smacked.

But there was another knock at the front door. *Bam bam bam!*

Josie Smith listened. She heard a voice. Mr. Scowcroft's voice. Mr. Scowcroft had come to tell on her for not wanting his eggs! She couldn't hear all the words, but she heard, "Took her scarf off and left it...," and then, "a couple of nice new-laid eggs...," and then, "But she ran off before I could catch her." Then the door banged. Mr. Scowcroft had gone away. Well, now she would *really* get smacked!

But there was another knock at the front door. *Bam bam bam!*

Josie Smith listened. She heard a voice. Mr. Kefford's voice. He'd come to tell on her for not wanting his apple!

She couldn't hear all the words, but she heard, "'I don't want that,' she said, the little monkey...," and then some words she couldn't hear and then, "But she ran off before I could catch her." Then the door banged. Mr. Kefford had gone away. Well, now she would really get smacked, and hard.

But there was another knock at the front door. *Bam bam bam!*

Josie Smith listened. She heard a voice. Mrs. Crawshaw's voice. She'd come to tell on her for running away from the horrible cactus plant!

She couldn't hear all the words, but she heard, "Thought she could buy two dozen roses for fifty cents! If you could have seen her face..." Josie Smith remembered how black the water was when she washed her face. Mrs. Crawshaw said some more words she couldn't hear, and then, "But she ran away before I could catch her." Then the door banged. Mrs. Crawshaw had gone away.

The light came on over the stairs and Josie's mom was standing at the bottom.

"You'd better come down," she said.

Josie Smith went down in her striped pajamas, holding the birthday card. If she gave her mom the birthday card first, perhaps she wouldn't get smacked so hard.

"Come into the kitchen," said Josie's mom.

Josie Smith went into the kitchen where it was warm.

"Look," said Josie's mom.

Josie Smith looked, and on the table was a bun with white icing and a cherry on top and two brown eggs with red speckles and a big, red, shiny apple and a beautiful, big, red rose and Josie's itchy scarf.

"Mrs. Chadwick's been here," said Josie's mom, "and Mr. Scowcroft and Mr. Kefford and Mrs. Crawshaw. They said I should be

proud of you because you wanted nothing but the best for your mom, but that you ran away before they could give you these things. Why did you run away?"

"I don't know," said Josie Smith.

"Well," said Josie's mom, "I've never had so many presents. I was only expecting a card and I thought you'd forgotten."

"I've made you a card as well," said Josie Smith, and she gave her mom the card with the big red roses on the front and the bun with white icing on it and a cherry on top and two brown eggs with red speckles and a shiny red apple inside and the letters in all different colors that said HAPPY BIRTH-DAY MOM.

JOSIE SMITH RUNS AWAY

On Friday afternoon, Josie Smith and Eileen were playing indoors because it was raining hard and Josie Smith had got wet coming home from school. Eileen hadn't been to school because she'd had German measles. They were playing dolls' hospital in Josie's bedroom.

"We have to take their temperatures," Eileen said.

Josie Smith got one of her crayons and held it near her big doll's mouth.

"I had my temperature taken," Eileen said, "and it was nearly a hundred."

Josie Smith held the crayon up and looked at it hard.

"This one's nearly two hundred," she said. Then she held it near the rag doll's mouth.

Eileen said: "My mom says you're going to get German measles as well."

"I'm not," said Josie Smith. "I only get tonsillitis."

"You are," Eileen said, "and you'll get spots. It's catching."

Downstairs, somebody knocked at Josie Smith's front door. *Bam bam bam!* Then Josie's mom shouted up:

"Josie! Gary Grimes wants to play!"

Josie Smith ran to the top of the stairs and shouted: "He can't play! We're playing dolls' hospital and he'll get rough and spoil it!"

But Gary Grimes was climbing up the stairs. His hair was wet and shiny and his ears stuck out.

"Your mom says I can play," Gary Grimes said.

"Well, you'll have to be sick then and not talk, and I have to take your temperature."

"I'll be the doctor," Gary Grimes said, "and shout in a big voice like Doctor

Gleason." And he started poking the dolls in the tummy.

"Get away!" shouted Josie Smith. "You're hurting them!"

"Don't be stupid," Gary Grimes said. "They're only dolls."

And they didn't play dolls' hospital anymore because Gary Grimes had spoiled it.

"I wish it'd stop raining," Josie Smith said, and she looked out of the window to see if it would. But the rain was splashing down harder than ever and all the stone houses in the street were black and wet and the slates on the roofs were dark and shiny and the rain bounced up from the dirty puddles. Behind all the rows of chimneys there should have been a hill with a tower on it, but the hill had disappeared in the clouds and that meant that it wouldn't stop raining today.

Josie Smith switched the light on because the rain made the house so dark and then she said, "Let's play school."

"Who'll be the teacher?" Eileen said.

"Me!" shouted Gary Grimes, jumping

and bouncing on Josie Smith's bed. "Me! Me!"

"I'm the teacher," Josie Smith said, "because I've got a new blackboard and easel."

Josie Smith pulled her blackboard and easel out from near the wardrobe and then she made Gary Grimes sit at one end of the bed and Eileen at the other end and all the dolls in a line in between them.

"Gary Grimes, stand up!" Josie Smith shouted.

Gary Grimes stood up.

"Say your two times table," Josie Smith said.

"One two is two, two twos are four."

"Stand up straight!" shouted Josie Smith.

Gary Grimes stood up straight, and when he'd finished his two times table Josie Smith made Eileen read out loud from a story book.

"There're big words in it," Eileen said.

"You have to read it and I'll help you," Josie Smith said, because she was best in the class at reading.

She made Eileen read a lot of hard words and then she said, "Sit down," and Eileen sat down.

Then Josie Smith wrote some letters very carefully across the top of her blackboard.

"Gary Grimes! Come here!" she said. Gary Grimes came. "Now," said Josie Smith, "copy these letters carefully underneath and don't let me see you rubbing out with your finger! And you have to do them in a straight line."

Gary Grimes made the chalk squeak and then he said, "I'm being the teacher now."

"No you're not," said Josie Smith, "because you're not clever enough."

But Eileen said, "We have to take turns, or it's not fair."

"It is fair," Josie Smith said, "because it's my blackboard."

"I'm going to call for Rawley Baxter," Gary Grimes said, and he ran off down the stairs.

"Nobody wants to play with you anyway!" Josie Smith shouted after him from the top of the stairs, "because you're soft!"

But when she came back into the bedroom, Eileen was undressing her bride doll.

"What are you doing that for?" Josie Smith said. "We're playing school."

"I'm not playing," Eileen said. "If you don't take turns it's not fair. And anyway, your blackboard's not new."

"It is."

"It isn't."

"It is. I only got it yesterday."

"I don't care. It's not new. It's secondhand. You can see all the scratches and shiny places on it."

Josie Smith got her eraser and started cleaning her blackboard. She cleaned it and cleaned it and cleaned it, but there were still scratches and shiny places on it. She hadn't noticed them before.

Then she smelled bacon frying downstairs and she said, "I'm going to have my supper, so you've got to go home."

But Eileen said, "I'm staying here for my supper. Your mom said so. And you're going to catch my German measles and get it over with."

"I'm not! And you're a pig!"

"A-aw! I'm telling on you for that. You're not supposed to say pig."

"Josie! Eileen!" shouted Josie's mom. "Wash your hands and come down!"

It was warm in the kitchen and they had bacon and baked beans and sausages and bread and butter and then some apple pie. Then they watched television and Josie Smith didn't speak to Eileen all the time because she hated her. When Eileen went back next door to her own house, Josie Smith said to her mom, "I don't want to catch Eileen's measles."

"German measles," said Josie's mom,

"and you're bound to catch them sooner or later so you might as well get it over with."

"But I don't want to catch them off Eileen. Why can't I catch them off Rawley Baxter's little sister?"

"You might."

"Can I go to their house tomorrow?" asked Josie Smith.

"We'll see," said Josie's mom.

"But can I?"

"I said we'll see."

"Why do you always say we'll see?"

"Because we shall have to see if you can go. Now get ready for bed."

"Mom," said Josie Smith, "what does second hand mean? Is it like a minute hand?"

"It's the smallest one," said Josie's mom. "The one that counts the seconds. Our clock hasn't got one, but your gran's big clock on the wall has. Now get ready for bed."

"Eileen said my blackboard and easel are second hand," said Josie Smith.

"That's different," said Josie's mom.

"Why is it different?"

"It means something different. It means somebody had your blackboard and easel before you."

"Who had it before me?"

"Nobody you know," said Josie's mom. "Now get ready for bed."

"It's got scratches on it, though, and shiny places where the chalk won't write. Eileen said."

Josie's mom went to the cupboard under the sink and got out a shiny red-and-white can. "What does that say?" she asked Josie Smith, giving her the can to read.

"Blackboard paint," read Josie Smith.

"Well, tomorrow morning we're going to paint your blackboard and then it'll be like new with no scratches or shiny places. Now get ready for bed and don't forget to brush your teeth."

When she was in bed and her mom came up to say good night, Josie Smith said, "I hate Eileen. She's horrible."

"Well, why do you play with her, then, if she's horrible?" asked Josie's mom.

"Because she's my best friend."

In the morning, Josie Smith woke up very early. She looked out the window, but it was still raining. Then she went to look at her blackboard and easel. She tried to write on it but the chalk squeaked and it wouldn't write on the shiny places, so Josie Smith went downstairs in her striped pajamas and got out the red-and-white can to read what it said. She forgot to put her slippers on and it was cold in bare feet so she took the can upstairs and got back in bed to read it. There were some big words in the instructions but Josie Smith read them all, even the ones she couldn't understand. Then she said to herself, "I've read all of it, so now I can paint my blackboard by myself. It's easy."

But when she tried to open the can, that wasn't easy and it hurt her nails and fingers. She got out of bed and shook a penny out of her piggy bank. When she pushed the penny under the edge of the lid, it came open. Josie Smith put her nose down near the black paint and sniffed.

"Oops..." she said when her nose touched the paint. "I bet I've got a black nose. When I've finished I'll have to get washed." Then she looked for a brush. She chose her biggest paintbrush but it wasn't really big enough, so she dug right down into the can and got as much of the sticky black paint as she could. "I'll start at the top," she said to herself and sploshed the lovely black onto the board on the top corner. It was very nice but it rolled down the board very fast and a long string of it went straight down to the floor. *Plop.*

"Oops," said Josie Smith, "I forgot to put some newspaper down." And she went downstairs to get some. Before putting it

down she tore a bit off and tried to mop up the blob on the floor, but it got bigger. "I'll have to clean it up when I've finished," she said, and she stood the blackboard and easel on the newspaper. "Oops..." she said, looking down at the front of her striped pajamas. There were red stripes and white stripes, and down one side there was a black stripe. "Well," she said, "I'll have to wash them when I've finished."

She went on painting until all the board was black and sticky and all the scratches and shiny places had disappeared. She stood back to have a good look at it.

"Oops..." said Josie Smith. Something had stuck to her foot. It was the upside-down lid of the paint can, and she had to sit down on the floor to unstick it and put it back on the can. Then she looked at the painted blackboard again and then she looked at herself. There was the long black stripe down the front of her pajama jacket and another long black stripe down her arm where the brush had dripped and two black hands and one black foot. Then she looked harder at the board and saw a row of drips falling off at the bottom. *Plop.*

"I'd better get washed," said Josie Smith, and she went to the bathroom. The soap turned black and the basin turned black and the towel turned black but Josie Smith stayed as black as ever. Josie Smith started worrying. And when she went back to her bedroom she started worrying even more because there was a line of small black footprints all the way from her room.

"I'd better clean everything up," said Josie Smith. So she rolled up the newspapers she'd put down and tried to get the black off the floor underneath and wipe up all the footprints, but the black marks didn't come off. They just got bigger. Josie Smith got frightened.

"I'll get smacked for this," she said to herself. And when she went back into her bedroom, the blackboard had started to drip again and there was no newspaper down anymore.

"Ooh..." whispered Josie Smith.

"Josie!" shouted Josie's mom from the other bedroom. "What are you doing?"

"Reading!" said Josie Smith, shutting her eyes tight because it was a lie. Then she started getting dressed as fast as she could. Outside her window it was still raining hard, *plop, plop, plop* into the puddles like the black paint from the bottom of the blackboard going *plop, plop, plop* onto the floor.

Josie Smith ran downstairs, put her rubber boots and raincoat on, and ran out the front door and off down the street as fast as she could go. But at the end of the street she stopped. She had to run away, but where could she run away to? Then she thought of her gran's house. That wasn't so far, so she wouldn't get very wet and her gran would let her play with the toys in the big drawer. So Josie Smith ran up the slope to the next street and in at her gran's front door.

"What are you doing here so bright and early?" asked Josie's gran from the kitchen.

"My mom told me to come," said Josie

Smith, shutting her eyes as tight as she could. "She's busy."

"Well," said Josie's gran, "you'd better get something to play with out of the big drawer, and then when it stops raining we'll go and do the shopping."

Josie opened the big drawer. There she found a paint box and some skittles and a spinning top and a jump rope and a lot of big, old books.

"If you want to paint," said Josie's gran from the kitchen, "I'll give you some newspaper."

"I don't want to paint," said Josie Smith.

"All right," said Josie's gran, "you do what you want. But you always say you like painting best."

"I don't like it today," said Josie Smith, and she got a big book out of the drawer and sat down on the rug.

"Take your boots off," called Josie's gran.

Josie Smith didn't want to take her rubber boots off because her sock was stuck to her foot where all the black paint was, but her gran was very old and she couldn't see very well, even when she had her glasses on. When she came in with her duster for a minute, she didn't even notice the black spot on Josie Smith's nose. So Josie Smith took her boots off and turned the pages of the big book in front of the fire.

She didn't like the big book as much as she usually did. Reading made her eyes hurt today and the fire felt too hot and she had a big lump in her throat from being frightened. When her gran said, "It's stopped, We'll go down to the shops," Josie Smith didn't want to go. She felt tired and she would have liked to lie down on the rug and go to sleep. But she put her rubber boots and her raincoat back on and went down to the shops with her gran.

"When we've finished the shopping," Josie's gran said, "we'll go and sit down in Mrs. Penny's and have some ice cream."

"I don't want ice cream today," said Josie Smith.

"Well," said Josie's gran, "that's funny. You always like ice cream."

"I don't like it today," said Josie Smith,

and the lump in her throat got bigger and bigger. Maybe her mom was looking for her. What would she do when she couldn't find her? Would she call a policeman? Would she cry? Josie Smith wanted to cry. She wanted to go home. And in a very tiny voice she said, "I think I want to be sick."

But it was a very, very tiny voice and her gran was busy talking to the butcher, saying, "And a quarter of minced..."

They went to the grocer's and the fruit

and vegetable shop and Josie Smith's legs felt tired in her rubber boots and the lump in her throat hurt and her chest was going *bump, bump, bump.* Then her gran took her to the ice-cream shop.

"I don't want any ice cream," said Josie Smith, "I feel sick." And she started to cry as loudly as she could.

Mrs. Penny leaned over the counter and said, "Whatever's the matter with our Josie today?" And she lifted up Josie Smith's chin.

"My word," said Mrs. Penny, "you're as black as coal! What have you been doing to yourself?" And she looked very hard at Josie Smith, and Gran bent down and *she* looked very hard at Josie Smith, and when Josie Smith stared back at them, their faces began to go round and round in the air.

"I feel dizzy," said Josie Smith, and all the ice-cream cones on the counter started going round and round, too.

Mrs. Penny's face went round and round, saying, "Spots on her forehead..." And her gran's face went round and round, saying, "I'd better take her home." Everything went dark in Josie Smith's head and then even the dark went round and round, and Josie Smith fainted.

When she woke up again, Josie Smith was in her own bed wearing clean striped pajamas and Doctor Gleason was listening to her chest and her mom's hand was pressing on her forehead all nice and cool. Doctor Gleason took the tubes out of his ears

and said in his loud voice, "She can get up in a couple of days if she feels like it. I'll leave you a prescription." Then he wrote on a paper and gave it to Josie's mom and they went off down the stairs and the front door slammed. *Bam!*

When Josie's mom came up again, Josie Smith said, "Am I sick?"

"Yes," said Josie's mom, "but you'll be able to get up in a day or two, the doctor said."

"Why are the curtains drawn?" asked Josie Smith. "It's morning."

"It's not morning," said Josie's mom. "It's seven o'clock and going dark."

"But I haven't had my breakfast," said Josie Smith, "and my lunch and my supper."

"You didn't want them," said Josie's mom. "Have you forgotten? You've been asleep a long time."

"I've forgotten," said Josie Smith. "Am I sick because I've been naughty?"

"No," said Josie's mom. "You're sick because you've got German measles."

"Have I got spots?" asked Josie Smith.

"All over your face and your tummy," said Josie's mom.

"And a temperature?" asked Josie Smith.

"And a temperature."

"Am I getting it over with?"

"That's right," said Josie's mom.

"And are they Eileen's measles?"

"They might be," said Josie's mom. "I don't know."

"But they must be somebody's, mustn't they? So they're secondhand." Josie Smith looked across to where her blackboard was. The black marks on the floor had gone and the blackboard looked like new.

"Even if they were Eileen's measles, they're mine now, aren't they? So even if you get something secondhand, it's still yours, the same as if it was new."

"Just the same," said Josie's mom. "I'll make you some hot lemonade now."

"And then will you tell me a story?"

"All right."

After the story was finished, Josie Smith said, "I was naughty for painting my blackboard, wasn't I?"

"No," said Josie's mom, "you shouldn't

have tried to do it by yourself but that was a mistake, you weren't being naughty."

"Not even when I spilled the paint?"

"Not even when you spilled the paint. That was an accident. You only did one naughty thing. You ran away."

"I won't do it again," said Josie Smith.

"I should think not," said Josie's mom, "and now you'd better go back to sleep."

The next day, Eileen came over from next door and brought Josie Smith a coloring book.

"I've only colored two of the pictures," Eileen said, "but you can have it because you're my best friend. My mom says you ran away."

"I did," said Josie Smith.

"Where did you go?" asked Eileen.

"Miles and miles away," said Josie Smith with her eyes shut. "On a bus."

"What did you run away for?" asked Eileen.

"Because I would have got smacked," said Josie Smith, "but now I can't get smacked because I've got German measles."

"I'm not scared of getting smacked," Eileen said.

"That's because your mom doesn't smack properly," said Josie Smith. "When my mom smacks she smacks *hard* and she can make stories up without a book and she bought me some special paint for my blackboard."

Eileen looked at the blackboard and she said, "It looks just like new."

"I painted it," said Josie Smith, "by myself."

"You never!"

"I did. Ask my mom. With thick black paint like syrup."

Eileen touched the blackboard with her finger.

"Didn't it spill on the floor?"

"Not much," said Josie Smith with her eyes nearly shut.

"Can I write on it?" Eileen said. And Josie Smith let her because even if Eileen was horrible sometimes, she was still Josie Smith's best friend.

JOSIE SMITH and GINGER

Josie Smith and Eileen were sitting on Josie Smith's doorstep cutting out. Gary Grimes was watching with his hands in his pockets.

"Let's play Cowboys and Indians," Gary Grimes said.

"We're not playing," Josie Smith said. "It's a boys' game."

"Well?" said Gary Grimes. "We played it yesterday."

Josie Smith and Eileen went on cutting out.

"I'm going to call for the boy at number ten," Gary Grimes said.

"There's nobody lives at number ten, stupid," Eileen said.

"There is," said Gary Grimes. "I saw the moving van this morning and there's a boy, bigger than me."

"He won't play with you, then," Josie Smith said, "because you're soft."

"Just you wait," Gary Grimes said. "I'll thump you if you say that again." Gary Grimes put his fist near Josie Smith's face and then he ran off down the street.

"Once he thumped me," Eileen said, "and I nipped him and then I told on him."

"You shouldn't nip," Josie Smith said.

And then Eileen's mom shouted, "Eileen! Eileen!"

"I've got to go in," said Eileen. "I'll call for you tomorrow to go to school."

Eileen went in. Josie Smith looked up the street and then down the street. There was nobody. The doorstep was cold but the sun shone down between the rows of chimneys and warmed Josie Smith's knees. She uncrumpled a piece of silver paper and spread it on her knee to smooth it out with her finger. When it was smooth she cut a star out of it. Josie Smith started smoothing out another piece of silver paper. Somebody sat

down on the step next to her. Somebody warm and furry who tickled her arm. Josie Smith put her paper and scissors down and looked around. There was a great big ginger cat with green eyes watching her. Josie Smith looked hard at the cat's face and the cat looked hard at Josie Smith's face. Josie Smith put her face a bit closer to the cat's face. Its big whiskers smelled of fish.

"What's your name?" Josie Smith said. "Is it Ginger?"

The cat blinked.

"I thought it was," said Josie Smith.

She felt his fur. It was shiny and warm.

"Eileen's gone in," she said. "You can play with me if you want."

Ginger blinked. Josie Smith put her arm round Ginger.

"You're a bit fat," she said. "Do you scratch?"

The place where the purr came out of his chest was white.

"I'll tell you a story if you want," Josie Smith said.

Ginger purred louder. Then he put two white paws on Josie Smith's knees and jumped.

"Oh!" said Josie Smith, "you're squashing me! Get down!" But Ginger didn't get down. He sat on Josie Smith's knee with his back to her and she couldn't see over his ears.

"You're knocking me down," said Josie Smith, struggling and pushing. "You're too big."

Ginger jumped down and sat next to her on the doorstep again, staring straight in front of him as if nothing had happened.

"I'd better not tell you a story," Josie

Smith said, "not if you have to sit on my knee for it. You're too big. You're nearly as big as me. Are you five?"

Ginger blinked. He washed both his front paws and his ears and one of Josie Smith's knees.

"It tickles," Josie Smith said. "You've got a funny tongue."

She put her tongue out at Ginger to see if he would put his tongue out at her so she could look at it but he only showed the very tip of it and squeezed his eyes shut.

Josie Smith did some more cutting out and Ginger watched. Then she felt hungry and thirsty.

"Wait for me," Josie Smith told Ginger. She put down her scissors and ran in at the front door and along to the kitchen. The kitchen smelled of washing and something boiling in a pan. The back door was open.

"I'm hungry and thirsty," Josie Smith said.

"Get some milk and cookies," said Josie's mom, and she carried some washing out into the yard.

Josie Smith poured the milk into a cup

and put three cookies on a saucer. Then she carried the cup and saucer out of the front door and sat down on the step again. Ginger was waiting.

"Here," said Josie Smith. She put the cookies on her skirt and poured half of the milk into the saucer.

Ginger looked at it. Then he crouched down very slowly and put his face near the saucer. He thought for a bit and then he poked his tongue out and began to lick up the milk.

"You were thirsty like me," Josie Smith said, eating her cookies. She broke a bit off one and held it out but Ginger twitched his nose and sat up straight, looking the other way.

"Why don't you like it?" Josie Smith asked him. "It's a ginger cookie." She left the piece on the step but Ginger didn't look at it.

The sun went behind a big cloud that covered all the sky between the chimneys.

"Josie! Josie!"

"I've got to go in," Josie Smith told Ginger. "Are you going in as well?"

Ginger didn't move.

"Haven't you got a house?"

Ginger didn't move.

"Are you lost?"

Ginger blinked.

"What are we going to do?" whispered Josie Smith. "I can't take you in with me because my mom'll shout."

"Josie! Josie!"

"I have to go in. You wait here and I'll ask my mom if I can have you."

"Wash your hands," said Josie's mom.

"I've washed them."

"Wash your hands," said Josie's mom.

Josie Smith washed her hands and sat down at the table. Her mom looked in a bad temper.

"Can we have a cat?" said Josie Smith.

"No," said Josie's mom.

"Why can't we?"

"Because we can't afford it."

"But if we don't buy one, if we just get one?"

"And what would it eat?"

"I'll give it some of my milk."

"Cats eat meat," said Josie's mom.

"And fish?" asked Josie Smith, remembering the smell of Ginger's whiskers.

"And fish, too. We can't afford it."

Josie Smith looked at her plate. There was a piece of meat on it and she didn't like meat. And poor Ginger was outside by himself with nothing to eat.

Josie's mom got up to cut some more bread. Josie Smith folded up the piece of meat and put it in her pocket.

"Can I have some jam?" said Josie Smith.

"Not until you've eaten your meat."

"I've eaten it," said Josie Smith, shutting her eyes when she said it because it was a lie.

"All right."

When she'd finished Josie Smith said, "Can I go out for a minute?"

"No," said Josie's mom. "It's getting dark."

It was getting very dark and it was starting to rain as well. Josie Smith could hear the rain pattering on the window behind the curtains.

Josie Smith waited until her mom started washing up and then got down.

"Where are you going?" said Josie's mom. "You can't play outside in the dark."

"I've left my cutting-out things on the doorstep," said Josie Smith, and she went and opened the front door.

"Miaow," said Ginger in the dark.

"Shh..." The street was black and shiny and the wind blew the rain in Josie Smith's face. She bent down and stroked Ginger. His fur was wet through and cold.

"You can't stay out here by yourself," whispered Josie Smith, and she felt the big lump coming in her throat to make her cry. She brought in her cutting-out things and got a knitted blanket off her dolls' carriage. She wrapped the blanket round Ginger and Ginger purred.

"Shh! I'll have to carry you," said Josie Smith.

Ginger was very heavy and his ears popped out at the top of the blanket and his whiskers tickled her nose and his wet tail popped out at the bottom of the blanket and tickled her legs but she managed to get him to the bottom of the stairs near the kitchen.

"What have you got there?" said Josie's mom, without looking.

"My doll," Josie Smith said, shutting her eyes tight.

"If you're going upstairs, put your pajamas on. It's late."

It was hard work getting Ginger up the stairs and three times Josie Smith nearly fell, but she got him into her room and shut the door.

Ginger jumped on Josie Smith's bed and his blanket fell on the floor.

"You'd better keep it on, Ginger," Josie Smith said. "You're wet through, you'll catch your death." That was what Josie's mom always said. Then she always said, "You'll have tonsillitis again."

Josie Smith covered Ginger up with the blanket again and gave him the meat from her pocket in little bits. Ginger chewed the bits, wagging his head. Josie Smith put her striped pajamas on and opened her bedroom door to shout.

"Mom?"

"I'm coming."

"You don't have to come up," shouted Josie Smith. "I can go to bed by myself. Eileen's mom doesn't come up."

"Eileen's mom has a baby to take care of."

"I don't care. I'm as big as Eileen and I can go to sleep by myself."

Josie Smith's mom said, "All right. But if you change your mind, shout for me."

But Josie Smith only shouted, "Good night!" and got into bed and switched the light off.

Down near her feet she could feel Ginger washing himself in the dark.

"Good night, Ginger," whispered Josie Smith.

In the morning Josie Smith woke up very early when her mom was still asleep. Ginger was still asleep as well.

"Wake up, Ginger," Josie Smith said. Ginger opened one eye and closed it again.

"You have to get up or my mom will catch you."

Josie Smith ran downstairs in her striped pajamas and pulled on her rubber boots to go out into the yard. In the coal shed there was an old wash basket that would make a good bed for Ginger. Josie Smith had to climb up on the coal to reach it and she got black all over. Then she dragged it upstairs to her room.

The noise woke Josie's mom.

"Josie! What are you doing up so early?" shouted Josie's mom from the other bedroom.

"Reading," said Josie Smith, and shut her eyes.

She put the doll's blanket in the basket and told Ginger, "You'll have to play outside while I'm at school." She opened the window and Ginger jumped down onto the wall in the yard.

"I'll bring you some lunch from school," Josie Smith promised him. "Good-bye, Ginger."

And every day when Josie Smith went to school she took a paper bag from the kitchen drawer folded up in her pocket, and into the bag she put the meat from her school lunch and on Fridays she put in a piece of fish. Josie Smith didn't like fish. Ginger liked fish very much. Every night he jumped up on the wall and in at the window and drank Josie Smith's milk and ate Josie Smith's school lunch. Then he went to sleep in his basket. Good night, Ginger.

Josie Smith told Eileen about Ginger because Eileen was her best friend. On

Saturday when they got some money to buy candy, they went to Mrs. Chadwick's shop and Josie Smith bought a can of real cat food for Ginger. Ginger purred.

On Sunday night, when Josie Smith had read Ginger a story and they were both ready to go to sleep, there was a knock at the front door. *Bam bam bam!*

Josie Smith heard a lot of voices and then she heard her mom's voice. "Josie! Come down!"

Josie Smith went down. There were a man and a lady and a big boy.

"Josie," said Josie's mom. "This is Mr. and Mrs. Earnshaw and Jimmy. They moved into number ten on Monday and they've lost their cat. Have you seen it?"

Josie Smith shut her eyes tight.

"Josie!"

Josie Smith shut her eyes tighter.

"Josie!"

Josie Smith squeezed her eyes shut so tight that she could see wiggly worms of light in the dark.

Then a voice at the top of the stairs said, "Miaow!"

"That's my Betsy!" said the big boy.

"No it's not," shouted Josie Smith, opening her eyes. "It's my Ginger!"

Ginger came down and Josie Smith got hold of him tight.

"It's my Ginger!" roared Josie Smith.

"It's my Betsy!" roared the big boy. And they both roared and cried and the grown-ups said, "A little girl called Eileen told Gary Grimes who comes to call for our Jimmy, and Mrs. Chadwick at the shop said she'd been in to buy a can of cat food."

And Josie roared and the big boy roared

and then they took Ginger away.

Josie Smith roared all the way upstairs and then she hid under the bedclothes and roared herself to sleep.

For a long time Josie Smith played by herself. She wasn't friends with Eileen because Eileen had told and she wasn't friends with Gary Grimes because Gary Grimes had told. One day, when Josie Smith was coming home from school by herself, Gary Grimes put his fist near her face and said, "You're a robber!"

"I'm not," said Josie Smith.

"You're a robber," said Gary Grimes. "You stole Jimmy Earnshaw's cat and his dad's a policeman and he's going to come to your house and get you."

Josie Smith ran all the way home and her rubber boots went so fast she couldn't feel the pavement but she could feel her chest going *bam bam bam!*

One day she saw Jimmy Earnshaw's dad coming out of their house in a black uniform and she ran away so fast she was nearly sick.

The next day, Gary Grimes put his fist up

near Josie Smith's face at playtime and said, "Jimmy Earnshaw's going to get you after school."

Josie Smith was the first to run out of the school gate, and she ran all the way up to her own street without stopping. But she heard somebody running behind her. Somebody bigger, running fast.

"Hey!" shouted Jimmy Earnshaw's voice behind her. "Wait!"

Josie Smith ran so fast that she tripped and fell, but she got up and ran even faster until she got home.

"Can I have a Band-Aid on it?" Josie Smith asked her mom when her knee was washed.

"It needs some ointment on it first," said Josie's mom. "You shouldn't run everywhere. Why can't you walk?"

When she went to bed Josie Smith unstuck one corner of the Band-Aid to look at her sore knee and then she stuck it back again.

Then there was a knock at the front door. *Bam bam bam!*

Josie heard Mr. Earnshaw's voice. Then she heard Mrs. Earnshaw's voice. Then she heard Jimmy Earnshaw's voice. Then Josie's mom shouted.

"Josie! Come down!"

Josie went down in her striped pajamas. There were Mr. Earnshaw and Mrs. Earnshaw and in between them was Jimmy Earnshaw holding out something very small and ginger in his hands.

"Our Betsy's had kittens," Jimmy Earnshaw said, "so we've brought you one. I tried to catch you after school to tell you but you're a fast runner."

Jimmy Earnshaw put the ginger kitten in Josie Smith's hands. It was warm and it stayed very still as though it were asleep.

"You can come and see the others, if you want," Jimmy Earnshaw said. "Come to our house tomorrow after school. Can you ride a bike?"

"Yes," said Josie Smith with her eyes shut.

"I'll let you have a ride on mine, if you want. I'll hold you on. My mom says our

Betsy would have wandered off if you hadn't looked after her. Sometimes, when you move, they go back to their old house and you never find them again."

Josie's mom was talking to Mr. and Mrs. Earnshaw. She didn't say, "We can't afford it."

When Mr. and Mrs. Earnshaw and Jimmy Earnshaw had gone, Josie's mom said, "We'd better warm some milk for it." And she stroked its fur.

"Eeh," said the kitten, and it put its face up with its eyes shut.

"Why doesn't it say miaow?" asked Josie Smith.

"It's too small," said Josie's mom.

"Is it too small to talk, like Eileen's baby?"

When Josie's mom was warming the milk, Josie Smith said, "Is Mr. Earnshaw a policeman?"

"No," said Josie's mom. "He's a postman."

The ginger kitten took a long time to drink its milk. Josie Smith carried it upstairs and put it in the big basket. Then she went to the top of the stairs to shout.

"Mom! Are you coming up to say good night?"

"I thought you were too big," said Josie's mom.

"I am," shouted Josie Smith, "but Ginger's only a baby!"

So Josie's mom came up.

"Good night, Josie Smith. Good night, Ginger."